JANE HUGHES has worked for
many years as a freelance
illustrator. She trained as a graphic
designer at Maidstone College of
Art, and subsequently worked as a
printmaker and lecturer while
developing her illustration career.
Her work has appeared in
advertising, magazines, and books
on packaging, and in many other
applications. Jane works in a
variety of media, of which oil
pastels are a great favorite.
She is also a keen sailor, gardener,
and kite-flyer.

Oil Pastels

WORKSTATION

JANE HUGHES

WORKSTATION *is a new concept comprising
all the elements you need to start
drawing with oil pastels.*

*The first 48 pages of the book offer a comprehensively
illustrated introduction to this rewarding pastime.
Included at the back of this book are 16 pages
of good quality cartridge paper to enable you
to begin sketching.*

PRICE STERN SLOAN
Los Angeles

A PRICE STERN SLOAN—DESIGN EYE BOOK

© 1993 Design Eye Holdings Ltd.
© Illustrations Jane Hughes

Produced by Design Eye Holdings Ltd.
First published in the United States by Price Stern Sloan, Inc.,
A member of The Putnam & Grosset Group, New York, New York.

ISBN: 0-8431-3758-4

3 5 7 9 10 8 6 4

Manufactured in China by Giftech Ltd.

Warning:
This product is intended as a beginner's guide for ages 8 and up.
Children under 8 years of age should be strictly supervised by an adult.
Conforms to ASTM D 4236-92

CONTENTS

INTRODUCTION

We live in a world filled with color and light, a wealth of visual excitement all around us. There are dozens, hundreds, of moments when something seen fleetingly makes a lasting impression to be filed away in the memory. Not only are we able to remember, however, we can also record those moments in drawings—the luminous sky at dawn or sunset, the subtle but brilliant jumbled colors of fallen leaves, or the softness of skin on the face of a sleeping child.

Color is perhaps the first quality we observe. For example, people usually can remember that the car they've seen is red, or that the coat they want to buy is blue. For many artists, color is the most exciting aspect of any drawing (including, perhaps paradoxically, monochromatic drawings). It is also a vital key to informing us and expressing our understanding of the world around us.

Pastel painting gives us a medium where we can draw (or "paint") with what are like fingers of pure color. There are two main types of pastel—soft pastels and oil pastels.

Soft pastels (sometimes called chalk pastels, or dry pastels) are made from colored pigment, sometimes bulked out with a little chalk. This is mixed with some gum as a binder, and the pastel is formed by compressing the pigment to make cylindrical sticks. These soft delicate chalks make wonderful rich velvety marks, with dense long-lasting color. Unfortunately the surface of the work can be damaged relatively easily.

Oil pastels, as their name implies, are made with an oil binder. This results in a pastel which is less fragile to handle than a dry pastel, and with several other characteristics which make them easy and versatile to use.

This workstation is devoted to drawing with oil pastels. The selection of pastels includes a good basic range of colors, which should enable you to make an enjoyable foray into working in the medium. It's not intended to be an intensive course of instruction, but I have set out to give a few simple guidelines about color and composition, and some ideas for subject matter. I have also included some less obvious ways of using oil pastels as a starting point for some experiments of your own. Now read on!

WHAT YOU NEED

Equipment and Materials

❖

First, a little more about oil pastels. They are a relatively new medium, invented not long after World War II as the result of collaborative experiments by Henri Sennelier, Henri Goetz, and Pablo Picasso. The three of them developed a new pastel with a consistency somewhere between a chalk pastel and a wax crayon.

[Note: There are many different types of oil- or wax-based crayons available, such as Crayola™ wax crayons, Oil crayons (much harder than oil pastels and thus smoother but less densely colorful), Oil sticks (oil paints in stick form), and Plastidecor™ (crayons made from a synthetic wax base). They are all well worth exploring.]

Oil pastels are made by boiling pigment together with an oil-soluble wax binder. This means that they are waterproof on paper and board, and set to a strong, permanent finish as they dry out. This drying is a very slow process, however, and may take years to complete, so it's a good idea to handle newly-done work with a little care, or even to use some Spray Fixative which helps to "set" the surface of the work.

Also useful are a roll of kitchen paper towels and a can of lighter fluid. As they are oil-based and rather waxy in texture, oil pastels are inclined to soften slightly in warm conditions, so your hands and anything else you touch can become very colorful! A piece of kitchen paper dampened with lighter fluid will clean pastel marks from most surfaces, including hands, without doing too much damage, and lighter fluid has further drawing uses as a solvent for the pastels. More about this later.

I like to have two Swann-Morton scalpels handy. I use a No. 10A blade for straightforward cutting of paper, "sharpening" the ends of pastels and for making some scraped marks.

I also use a No. 15 blade which is curved. I find this is better than the 10A for working on larger areas of pastel, say as a preliminary for erasing part of the work, as it is less inclined to dig in its sharp point into the paper. Either blade works just as well—it's simply a matter of preference, and both can be used for Sgraffito. Scalpels and blades are easily obtainable from art suppliers.

You may want to erase part of a drawing, and it is possible to clear most if not all of an unwanted section. I find that scraping away the worst, followed by work with a good firm plastic eraser, will do the job well; however, I think it's generally better to work around, or over, or even simply to live with a "mistake."

Here is a selection of materials; as you can see, oil pastels come in many shapes and sizes.

Supports

❖

The choice of further equipment depends upon what you are trying to achieve in your work. Your choice of supports to work on, for instance, is almost limitless.

You can buy different qualities of paper, both in pads and—for a much wider selection—in single sheets. Good quality paper (handmade, watercolor, etching) can be expensive but is lovely to work on and often more durable. Cartridge paper, even cheap brands, is an excellent choice for general pastel work, but try using colored papers, or interestingly textured papers. It can even be fun to work on materials such as wallpaper or newspaper, or even paper bags.

Here I've tried out a few pastels to see how they appear on various textures and colors. All sorts of materials can be used as supports for oil pastels. Be adventurous and discover for yourself which surfaces are good to work on, and which achieve interesting results.

You don't have to limit yourself to paper as a support. Oil pastels will mark on most surfaces including canvas, cardboard, metal, wood, glass, plastics or leather, although with varying degrees of success and permanence. Give your imagination full rein!

Know Your Pastels

❖

Whenever I buy a new set of colors, whether paints, pencils, or pastels, I always try out each one to see exactly how they turn out on paper. Names and wrappers can confuse, and there's nothing like a real sample of a color to give an idea of its qualities.

On this page, I have worked up samples of each color in your set using the pastels just as they come from the pack. I have used both smooth white paper and a slightly rougher black paper, and have also varied the strength of mark (light and heavy).

White paper shows the true color of the pastels, and gives an idea of their relative strength.

A dark base color such as black alters the contrast of colors, intensifying deeper colors and lifting the lighter colors.

This exercise gives a useful indication of the way each color looks against either a light or a dark background, and also of their density.

You can make good use of the way colors advance or recede against each other to enhance the impression of depth in your pictures.

❖

On this page, I have again drawn up the colors, but this time I have begun a sequence of trial color mixes by overlaying each sample with single different colors, in this case blue, red, and white.

This exercise (which of course *you* could repeat for each color) gives an idea of how the colors can be overlaid to mix further colors. It can become a continually expanding project as you enthusiastically buy more oil pastels, available in a wide range of irresistible colors!

Making Marks

❖

If you have made some sample color drawings, you will have begun to get used to the feel of oil pastels. The marks you make can be modified with your fingers, or with knives or brushes, or with solvents and heat.

While the size of an oil pastel may suggest that it's not the ideal implement for drawing fine detail, it is possible to work on a large support so that the marks you make can show a wider range of scale.

• Try varying the pressure you use to alter the character of a line.

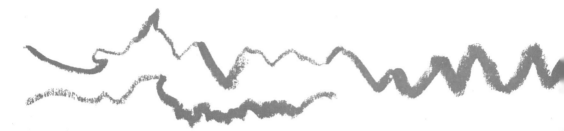

• Perhaps sharpen the end with a knife.

• Or peel off the wrapper and use the long side for broader marks.

• Try using a textured surface under the paper and make rubbings (**Frottage**).

• Or smudge and blend colors with your fingers or with kitchen paper.

• Apply some lighter fluid with à brush or cotton ball to make a wash.

• Try building the surface thickly and then scraping parts of it away (**Sgraffito, Grattage**), either with a blade or pencil.

Fixative can be useful when building up layers in a drawing as it will set the work quickly, making it possible to draw on top without necessarily altering the first layer.

It is exciting that there are so many ways to use oil pastels. Strictly speaking, the pastels and paper provided here are all that is required to begin with, but as you progress and become accustomed to the feel and characteristics of oil pastels, I hope you will find that the techniques and equipment suggested here will prove to be helpful.

Oil pastel is a bold and expressive medium. Be expansive and enjoy it!

WHAT TO DRAW...

Sketchbooks

❖

The best reason for making a drawing is that you really want to draw. That enthusiasm invariably communicates itself through the resulting work, and the subject assumes a sense of importance which the viewer may not have recognized or even considered.

The subject you choose to paint might be a straightforward representation of a favorite place, or perhaps a portrait of a friend. You might be more interested in showing some of the beauty of flowers and plants, or a walk through rainy streets just as the lights are being switched on in the evening. You may even prefer to draw a new pair of shoes still in the box.

Sketches are invaluable for instantly capturing the essence of a subject, and for making visual and verbal notes for use at a later date.

If you don't already regularly use a sketchbook, I hope this set will encourage the habit. It is so useful as a source of reminders and ideas in addition to its function as a practice pad.

Sketchbooks can often be more interesting than "finished" pieces, showing very directly the thinking and feeling of the artist, and keeping alive the spontaneity of the work. Very much a matter of personal taste, they are available in a huge choice of formats and it's a good idea to have a range of sizes—from your constant pocket companion to a larger size pad, say A2 (16.54 inches x 23.39 inches).

This workstation is an excellent format for the artist on the move. You have a good selection of your chosen medium, oil pastels, packaged in a strong book which doubles as a makeshift drawing board for the paper included in the set.

Use your sketchbook as a treasure chest for ideas and inspiration. It doesn't have to be exclusively for drawing in; it can become a combination of diary, datebook, and scrapbook as well. Often there is only time to make a few quick marks to record what you see, to be taken away and worked on later. Make notes to give yourself more information about textures, color, even how you feel about what you are drawing. Collect pictures from magazines, and, of course, you can always take and use your own photographs.

Your sketchbook will develop into a personal inspiration bank. Visual material is invaluable as reference which can be used at a later date. Drawing in your sketchbook, particularly with oil pastel, will make you want to go as to develop more expansive ideas.

Sketchbook pages drawn on a riverside walk one sunny May afternoon.

It's very enjoyable to change the scale of your work. If you want to work big and you don't have an easel, you could improvise by propping a drawing board against a chair, or taping your paper to a door (preferably an unpaneled door ...).

It is interesting to explore details of your subject matter, such as the coarse texture of an old stone wall or the grain of a piece of timber. Look for the intricate patterns in natural forms, fish scales, plant structures, crystals. Observing and drawing these structures will reveal the strength and beauty of their natural design, a constant source of inspiration for so many artists.

I drew a larger version of this boat as I particularly liked the soft colors of the old paint on the boat, and the glistening mud.

The man made world is just as captivating. The engine of a vintage car, a wrapper from some sweets bought on a foreign vacation, paint peeling from a post in a boat yard—all these have their own special beauty, or some story to tell. Don't feel, though, that you always have to record faithfully what you see in front of you.

The importance of looking carefully and intelligently at your subject as you draw is vital, but it is often more what you choose to include or exclude that makes a successful picture. Sometimes, it is more important to concentrate on one small part of a drawing, leaving the rest "unfinished." In any case, make your work reflect the reason you wanted to do it. Whether it is the colors that spurred you to draw or the complex structure, or even the atmosphere of the particular moment, that enthusiasm will shine through in your work.

I drew this boat from earlier sketches I made.

Remember, there is interest to be found in even the most commonplace things, if you only look, and drawing is probably the most exciting way of discovering it.

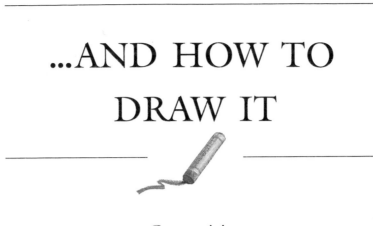

...AND HOW TO
DRAW IT

Composition

A s with any drawing medium, the techniques used for oil pastels
become very personal to the artist. I usually begin using a pale or
neutral color pastel sympathetic with the main colors in the subject, and
draw in loose guidelines to establish the composition of the picture.

There are rules for the composition of images, which were devised
during the Renaissance, and were then developed and handed down to
the present day. The conventions demonstrated by these rules have
become such an integral part of Western visual culture that most people
have a firm idea of what looks "right" without even realizing it.
Nonetheless, it is a good idea to try and develop some awareness of
good composition. Look at work by the Old Masters, and by painters
working today. Don't be overawed! Just try to recognize what makes
their paintings so successful.

*Generally, very symmetrically placed
elements tend to make for a static
composition.*

*Leading the eye through the composition to
your center of interest gives your picture
more flow, and makes it more involving.*

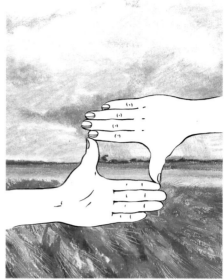

Use a cardboard viewfinder to frame your chosen area.

Alternatively you can use your hands like this to achieve the same effect.

It may be helpful to make a cardboard viewfinder (by cutting two L-shaped pieces of card as shown above) with which you can isolate areas of your subject, whether large landscape or still life. You can then see which section interests you most.

Another way of "framing" is to use your hands as shown above— much as film directors do.

Don't be afraid to adapt what you are drawing to suit the composition you want. As you gain more confidence in your own judgement, you will see that these rules of composition are only for guidance, and, with artist's license, you can contradict the conventional approach, often with exciting results.

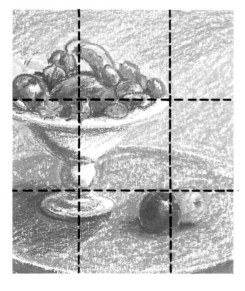

The "rule of thirds" suggests that where the dotted lines cross are good positions for your center of interest (perhaps not all at once though ...).

Another excellent variation is to try framing your subject closely (cropping). Large shapes should be balanced against small, empty areas against "busy."

Perspective

The problem of trying to represent our three-dimensional world in two dimensions is fundamental to drawing. If you draw **exactly** what you **see**, and not what you **know**, or **think** you see, you will automatically draw things correctly in perspective. However, it is not always easy to visualize without the objects in front of you.

What you see in these pages is very basic information about perspective. For further information, there are many excellent books devoted entirely to the subject. Remember that perspective is a means of checking the accuracy of your drawing, particularly when working from your imagination.

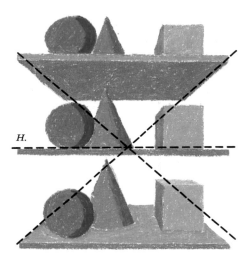

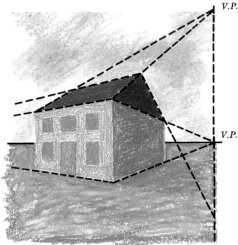

H is the Horizon or Eye Level (always at the eye level of the artist whether standing or sitting). Drawing your subject from above or below is a good way to add interest.

Parallel lines appear to converge at a Vanishing Point (V.P.) which is on the Horizon, or above or below the Horizon for inclined planes.

Circles need not cause problems to the artist. They and other awkward shapes including figures can be plotted by drawing squares around them in perspective.

Objects appear fainter and smaller as distance increases. Reflections will appear directly below their subject and at the same size (but in mirror image of course).

V.P.

H.

Eye level

This drawing shows a more complicated series of perspective features. Standing on the lawn, my natural eye level made a horizon line apparently just above the steps, the trees and hedges nearest to my viewing point all having planes with vanishing points on H. Beyond the hedge, the rising ground plane and the two rows of trees made a second horizon, or upper horizon, with another vanishing point, which I established in the drawing by aligning the bases of the trees. Use the rules to help—not to stifle—your work. You will learn more about perspective from your own observation than from anything else.

Color

❖

The theory of color perception is a vast and fascinating subject, which rewards further investigation. Here, as a start, is some very basic information.

Visible light, which is what mostly illuminates our world, can be broken down into the spectrum of colors from red to violet, as in a rainbow. Objects reflect white light rays in different ways so that, for instance, a tomato absorbs most of the white light spectrum but reflects the red part so that we see it as red.

Shown below is a color wheel showing the relationships of pigment colors as we see them. (Colored light is a rather different matter for which, regrettably, there is not enough space here).

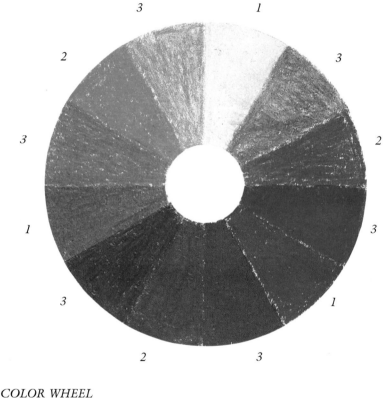

THE COLOR WHEEL

1 PRIMARIES	*2 SECONDARIES*	*3 TERTIARIES (clockwise)*
Yellow	*Orange*	*Yellow-Orange*
Red	*Violet*	*Red-Orange*
Blue	*Green*	*Red-Violet*
		Blue-Violet
		Blue-Green
		Yellow-Green

Colors can be darkened with black (hues) or lightened with white (tints).

The primary colors form the basis of all the other colors in the spectrum. Two primaries can be mixed to make a secondary color, and adding the third primary to that secondary will make a tertiary color. An infinite range of intermediate colors can be mixed thereafter.

COMPLEMENTARY COLORS

The colors immediately opposite each other on the color wheel are known as **complementary** colors. These opposing colors can be used very effectively to emphasize each other's particular characteristics in a drawing, much as black and white can be used to make dramatic contrast, for example.

Notice how complementary colors tend to intensify each other when juxtaposed, but how their mixture makes a neutral color (a sort of "brown").

Here the three primary colors are shown first adjacent to, and then blended with, their complementary colors. This shows how complementary colors intensify each other and how mixing them can make a neutral intermediate color.

ANALOGOUS (HARMONIOUS) COLORS

Analogous colors are those on the wheel which share the same primary, making a harmonious family of colors. Their complementaries appear on the opposite side of the wheel, and therefore make for a contrast in "temperature" as well as color. This is a useful quality to exploit to great effect (in drawing shadows, for example).

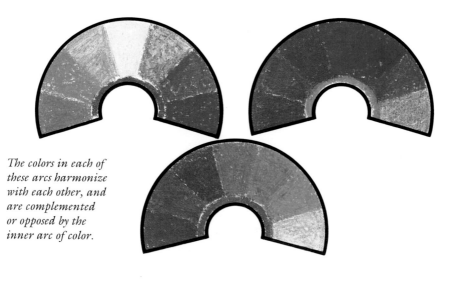

The colors in each of these arcs harmonize with each other, and are complemented or opposed by the inner arc of color.

Measuring

❖

In the early stages of any drawing, I try to get the proportions right, measuring by using a pastel, or pencil, or stick, (or even just my fingers) in the time-honored fashion.

This always looks like a rather a mysterious procedure if you don't know how to do it, so here is a brief explanation.

Hold a pencil or stick of some sort (or just use your thumb) vertically at arm's length so that you can use it to measure against the object you are drawing. For example, measure off the size of the head of your subject. It goes into the height of the body three times in this view. Now, looking at your paper, make a rough drawing to indicate the size of the head and then draw the body. This should be three times the measurement of the head you have just drawn. Using this same procedure, measure all the dimensions you need such as the width of a face, distance between the features, length of limbs, and so on.

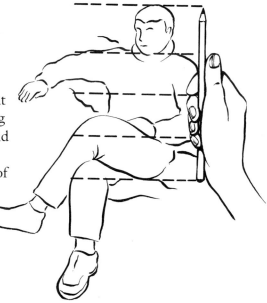

Use a pencil to set out the proportions of your subject by measuring one part of the body against another.

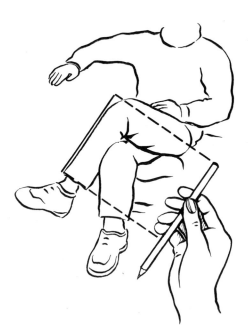

Check that you have drawn the limbs at the right angle by using a pencil as a parallel guide.

You can also check that you have angled the body and limbs correctly by using your pencil like a pointer to follow the direction of the various parts of your subject. Use any background features to help position your subject, and check that the vertical and horizontal features match up in both the subject and your drawing. Find a way to measure which suits you—measuring is essential for accurate drawing, whatever the subject. In time, you will find that it becomes easier to judge dimensions and that usually when you measure your work, it is right first time!

After making my initial guideline drawing, I then outline, or block in, the colors in their correct positions. From this point onward, the drawing can become either very free and open, or more densely worked, with areas of detail and contrasting broad statements.

In this drawing I began with a light outline sketch in the appropriate colors, and I have started to work more into the figure, having established the framework of the drawing.

Colored pencils are useful for adding finer detail, cutting through layers of pastel in a Sgraffito technique. Pencils, chalks or charcoal, (either black or colored), can also be used for initial underdrawing. The contrasting textures of the dry powdery chalky marks and oil pastel can be used to good effect.

Mixing Media

❖

Sometimes I use a mixture of media. It's interesting to use oil pastels as a watercolor resist, and to experiment with unusual wax- or oil-based colors such as metallics and fluorescents. These techniques can all add variety and richness to your work.

For the mixed media drawing on the opposite page, I worked on paper which I stretched by soaking it with water and then sticking it to a board with gummed paper tape round the edges. This stops the paper buckling when using watercolor washes. Once the stretched paper was dry, I began by outlining the shells with white, blue, gray, and mauve oil pastels. I then used strong pastel watercolor washes to exaggerate the natural colors of the shells. With white oil pastel I then drew the light areas of the figured marble surface the shells were resting on, before painting on a wash of blue watercolor. The oil pastel drawing repels the watercolor, giving an interesting, almost irridescent, effect.

As a change from full color, it can sometimes be interesting to restrict yourself to working in one color, but perhaps using a combination of different media.

The subtle difference in quality of materials can add interest to your work, and you can use a wide tonal range of a single color, (e.g. black through grays to white) to great effect.

Here's a black and white drawing where I used a mix of black charcoal and gray oil pastels.

You can also join together parts of separate drawings, or work on a support made of papers and fabrics layered together. It might be interesting to draw a landscape where you have made rubbings of bark as a base to work on, with the added textures of, say, canvas and sandpaper in addition to straightforward paper or card.

For this drawing I made rubbings from wood, hardboard, concrete, corduroy, and a power abrasive disc. These I collaged together to make a base drawing of the field onto which I drew the flames and smoke of the stubble fires.

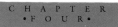

GETTING TO GRIPS

Every drawing has its testing bits, and there are no real short cuts or easy answers to get you out of these difficulties. This is not meant to be discouraging; on the contrary, it is precisely the challenge of this difficulty which makes drawing so tremendously satisfying.

The remarks which accompany the images on the next few pages are not intended to be "rules" or even directions. They are simply points which I have noted in my work, and which I hope will be helpful to you.

Landscape

With landscape drawing, there is much to consider in terms of scale and the particular aspect you are trying to convey. In the drawing below, I made a series of lighter fluid washes to build up the cloudy sky, putting the colors down in solid blocks which I then spread with lighter-fluid-soaked kitchen paper. Light base colors for the field were then applied in the same way, and then layers of pastel built over them to give a feeling of density. The trees on the horizon were drawn loosely to enhance the impression of distance, and lastly I drew in the barley whiskers by scraping through the layers of pastel with a scalpel.

The effects of light and shade are important in conveying the atmosphere of a landscape.

Distance alters our perception of color, softening and fading toward the horizon with the effects of aerial perspective. The interplay of texture and color can make some parts of the image appear to recede or to stand out, a small spot of localized color assuming greater significance than the rest of the picture.

The effects of light and shade are immensely important in conveying the atmosphere of a landscape. By looking toward the sun, as in the drawing shown above, the trees are seen almost in silhouette, giving them a flattened, slightly mysterious quality. The warm but subdued color palette gives an autumnal afternoon feeling, with even a hint of melancholy.

Contrasts of light and texture in this landscape are brought out by the use of Sgraffito *and wash techniques.*

Architecture

❖

The strong colors and dense texture of oil pastels help to convey the solidity of bricks and mortar. Try using washes to cover larger areas, building on them with layers of color to emphasize the surface and details. As with landscape drawings, the atmosphere, lighting, and time of day can dramatically alter the look of the place you are drawing. As with any subject matter, the particular facet of a building that you are trying to convey will govern how you approach the drawing. I am often as interested in small details of buildings as much as by the whole structure, and I find that sketches done on site, or photographs taken for reference are helpful for working on later in making more complex drawings. The drawing below was developed from sketches and photographs taken on a very cold but bright wintery day, when it was much too cold for sitting outside to draw!

The Royal Pavilion, Brighton. I used lighter fluid washes and light work with pastels, tied together with graphite pencil.

These pillars have a satisfying weight and solidity which is brought out by the density of thick layered oil pastel.

I drew this facade from the opposite side of a busy street in New York. I love the varied window shapes and the lurid colors!

It's not always appropriate to "fill in" your drawing. Sometimes a linear approach can express more succinctly what you want to convey in your drawing.

Liverpool Street Railway Station, London. This vaulted roof has a vitality and rhythm which almost contradict the immensity of its function. By leaving some undrawn areas of paper, the feeling is maintained of air and space between the spans of the roof.

The Nearer Landscape

❖

I find much inspiration in the more close-up "landscapes" we all see every day—the stalls and barrows in markets, shop windows, and awnings, and the chance arrangements of things like building materials. It's interesting to approach this day-to-day subject matter with a fresh eye.

The colors of the fruit on this open air stall were ideally suited to an oil pastel treatment, with emphasis on the contrasting colors and textures.

The bold blue stripes of the deckchairs are emphasized by the bright sunlit white stripes. This contrast was made all the stronger by not drawing the white stripes but leaving the paper blank, and by making a soft pastel colored background.

Try working in a less descriptive, less literal way. See how your subject can be analyzed into groupings of color, or areas of tone or texture. Work in the complementary colors to those that you can actually see (refer back to the color wheel). It may not produce a conventional looking image, but it will be an interesting exercise in the use of color, and may well open other avenues of exploration.

I am fascinated by the way in which shopkeepers set out their wares, in seemingly complex, carefully worked-out displays. I love to see the patterns which evolve from the logical and practical arrangement of goods in their packaging, or on shelves, and the rich variety of color and texture.

The rich colors of these sweaters make an intriguing, almost abstract image.

Similarly, the magazines and papers on this stand create a striking arrangement.

Still Life

❖

Moving in closer, still life is probably my favorite subject area. I like to draw things which tell some story about themselves, whether directly or by association. Souvenirs from a holiday, equipment for a hobby, a collection of stones and shells from a seaside walk—all make wonderful material from which to work.

The drawings shown here demonstrate different approaches to still life as a subject. The first one is a real holiday souvenir, a record of two memorable ice cream specials. The drawing was developed from very hasty sketches, with reference to the little flags and parasols (kept after the ice cream was eaten) and from a photograph taken at the time. The colors were applied solidly but leaving some bare paper to bring out the brightness of the late morning sunshine. The background was kept dark with little detail to add to the brightness of the ice creams.

The contrast between the deep, flat color of the background and the bright detail of the ice creams makes a lively composition.

A drawing of cabbages to suggest the drawing process.

I also enjoy drawings which make some comment, or even some sort of visual pun upon their subject. This second drawing is a drawing about drawing a drawing. It is a drawing of a drawing in progress, which is why it is apparently unfinished, and why it includes a drawing of the oil pastels which made the drawing. The cabbages themselves were initially drawn for their rich color, and the preliminary outlines and sequence of development of the drawing suggested the idea of making an image about the drawing process.

This drawing is purely and simply about the rich color of these Victoria plums!

People and Other Animals

When drawing people, try to decide what gives the strongest impression of their character. This might be their coloring, or a particular feature, the way they move or even the clothes they are wearing. The human figure is often thought to be difficult to draw, probably because most of us think we know what people should look like, so it's hard to get away with inaccuracies! Don't be put off, just keep practicing and your work will improve dramatically.

This saddle-maker very kindly sat while I made several sketches and notes for this portrait. The sketches gave basic information about color and form, and I also took some photographs for reference.

This drawing, an early stage of the final portrait, shows my first outline drawing, done in the appropriate colors. I have started to work into the eyes and the nose suggesting some overall color.

Here the eyes are almost completed, as is most of the face, leaving only the hair, beard and clothes to be finished. I decided early on with this drawing that I was not concerned with drawing the background at all, thus giving the subject undivided attention.

Try drawing parts of figures—hands, or head-and-shoulder portraits perhaps. With moving subjects, such as animals, quick sketches showing form and mass help to give an understanding of how the body works.

This cat seemed to be having a good time climbing repeatedly over a pile of logs (I think it was hunting mice). This meant that I had several opportunities to try and capture it on its circuit. It also stood, as shown here, watching some birds in a nearby hedge for several minutes, which made it much easier to draw!

Take advantage of a moment's stillness of your subject. I drew this cat with large loose strokes using the side of a pastel, drawing together the markings later.

The effect of the light was captured here by building the image gradually with very light pastel strokes.

The two drawings here are largely concerned with the effects of light on form. The drawing on this page is described as a ***contre-jour*** (against the light) drawing. The semi-silhouette quality serves to accentuate the form of the neck where the light floods over the shoulders. The light filtering through the bougainvillea growing over the balcony gives a warm dappled glow to the stone floor, diffusing and softening the folds of the shirt hanging on the chair

The drawing of the lady on the mule is a good example of how shade can be as descriptive as light. The faded colors of the buildings give little clue to the temperature or the time of the day, but the shadows cast by the balconies, canopies and mouldings, and by the lady's parasol, make strong contrasts, creating dramatic emphasis.

Working over several lighter fluid washes, the drawing was strengthened with dense pastel marks, and some loose detail was drawn in pencil.

Flowers

❖

Oil pastels really come into their own when one is painting flowers. You can capture the delicate character of petals with a soft wash of color, strengthening the form with direct strokes of the pastel. I like to vary the degree of detail I draw, sometimes concentrating on just a single flower head, sometimes making a much broader, freer drawing.

For the drawing below, shown in three stages of development, I chose a dull green Ingres paper. Its surface has a lined texture (known as "laid"), and the strong color makes a dramatic background for the white daisies.

(Step by Step)

I began this drawing by positioning the yellow centers and blue flower heads, using simple pastel strokes.

Then I added the white daisy petals and some of the lighter and darker stems.

I continued adding to the stems, then finally put in a little more detail and some seed heads.

This drawing of a magnificent flower stall
was made by blocking in loose areas of each
color, and then by simply working more
detail into each area. The cellophane was
drawn with heavy layers of white oil pastel
and wax crayon.

There is great dramatic effect in the massing of flowers or plants, and in the grouping and contrast of their colors and textures into almost abstract patterns. By moving in close (and perhaps "unfocusing" your gaze) you can present your subject in a new light. The unfamiliar scale and viewpoint of a close-up can be very exciting, as well as being very descriptive of textures and structures.

By simplifying the shape and limiting the colors used, the character of the snowdrops is expressed very directly.

These poppies have an intense dramatic quality accentuated by the thick heavy (impasto) pastel treatment.

By contrast, the pale washes and soft delicate pastel work on this pink poppy show the lightness and fragility of the petals, vividly offset by the black center of the flower.

Pattern

Don't forget that painting has a vital function as decoration. The wealth of pattern all around us, both in nature and in the manmade world, has been a source of inspiration since people began to draw. The camouflage markings of animal hides, the complex patterns and colors of butterfly wings and birds' feathers make wonderful rich subjects.

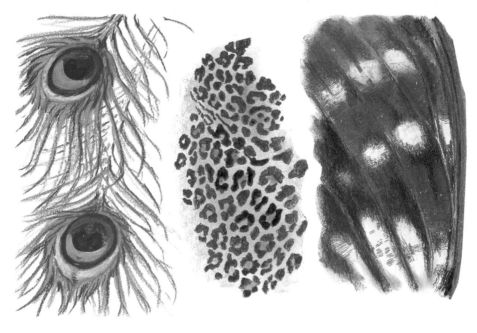

Peacock Feathers   *Leopardskin*   *Butterfly Wing*

Patterns abound in manmade form, from simple symmetrical structures like hinges to complex repeating designs, such as brickwork or tiles. The differing qualities of materials add to the visual excitement of the patterns around us. Metals, ceramics, and textiles have very different characteristics which can provide inspiration.

Roofing Tiles

Rope Mat

Brass Hinge

Patterns derived from all sorts of sources have been developed into designs for countless objects. Metal, woodwork, textiles, ceramics, paper goods—all are given decorative treatments by applying patterns. All this surface design and texture can be incorporated into complex imagery or simply enjoyed as exciting and beautiful in its own right.

Indian Bird kite

Sanjo Rokkaku fighting kite

*Japanese Carp windsock,
flown on the birth of a boy*

Takuma Semi Cicada kite

Tukkal Indian fighting kite

Nagasaki Hata fighting kite

Juggling Ideas

❖

Rather than trying to draw something so it looks "right," as you know it should look, drawing *precisely* what you see can often give some interesting results. Reflective surfaces, figured glass and the effects of light can distort objects in fascinating ways.

A kettle is a familiar object which has the ability to change the way we see other familiar objects. I have drawn this kettle to show how its curved sides can distort the images reflected, offering a starting point for some new ways of looking at drawing.

The form of the subject can also be manipulated, perhaps to show similarities or contradictions of texture and substance. You could make a series of drawings showing the metamorphosis of one object into another, making use of a wide range of marks and supports.

The Robot and Teddy Bear shown here share several characteristics: they are both about the same size, both walk upright on two legs, and both have recognizable faces. I drew two transitional stages as an investigation into how an object might change from one quality to another.

Letterforms and other graphic symbols provide rich pickings for visual development. Words lend themselves to illustrative treatments, and as simultaneously informative and decorative elements in a picture. Letters have a particular beauty in their own right, combining subtlety of form with the strength of their familiar meaning.

This drawing is based on the patterns seen in a stack of boxes (containing Squash balls). The colors on the boxes were changed in an arbitrary way so as to break down the organized typographic format and to create a near abstract colored surface. Letterforms and graphic elements make up the visual texture.

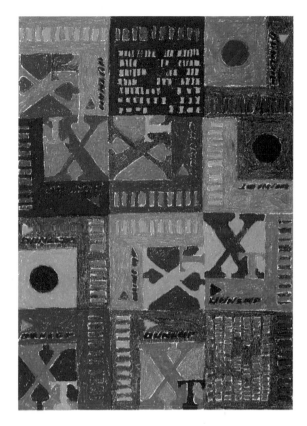

CONCLUSION

IHOPE YOU HAVE ENJOYED this introduction to oil pastel painting, and that it has given you some ideas to develop for yourself. However, I firmly believe that reading a book about drawing can only ever be an introduction, and that you will make the most progress in drawing by actually doing it. Don't be put off if your first efforts do not quite meet your exacting standards. Just keep going!

Remember, painting and drawing, however hard the struggle to "get it right" (which you will!), is supremely rewarding. More importantly, it is fun and satisfying. There is so much to learn from the work and ideas of other artists, but even better, so much you will discover entirely for yourself.

Enjoy your work!